The Further Adventures of

The QUEEN MUM

Also by Harry Hill

TIM THE TINY HORSE

The Further Adventures of

The QUEEN MUM

Harry Hill

ff

FABER AND FABER

For Mum, Happy Seventieth

First published in 2007
by Faber and Faber Limited
3 Queen Square London WC1N 3AU

Printed in the United Kingdom by Butler and Tanner, Frome

Design by Faber

A CIP record for this book
is available from the British Library

ISBN 978–0–571–23601–5

2 4 6 8 10 9 7 5 3 1

Sadly, at the age of 101, the
Queen Mum passed on from this life . . .

WAY
IN

GOD took the Queen Mum to one side
and told her he had someone to introduce
her to . . . someone very special . . .

. . . her old friend **King George VI.**

They had an
emotional
reunion at the
nightly
heaven
DISCO.

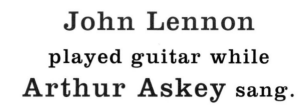

John Lennon
played guitar while
Arthur Askey sang.

Keith Moon played
drums and Kurt
Cobain did harmonies.

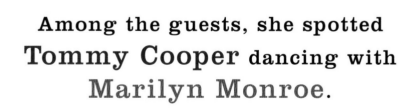

Among the guests, she spotted
Tommy Cooper dancing with
Marilyn Monroe.

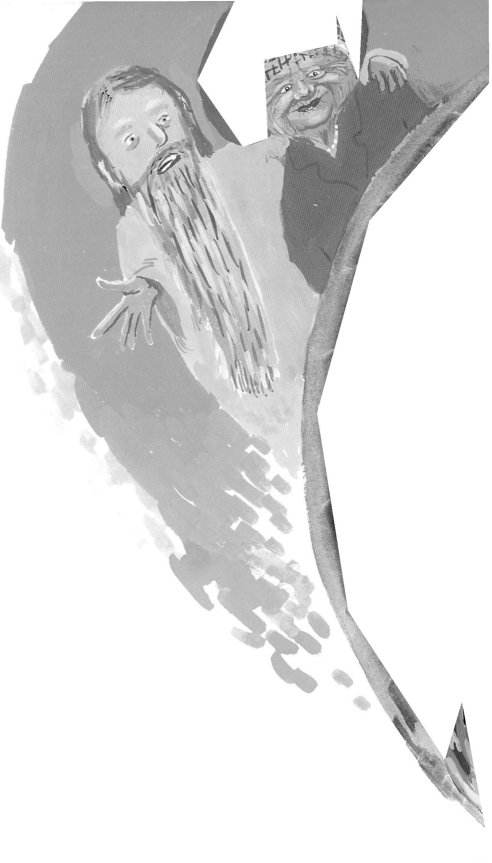

She was pleased to see that there was no place in heaven for her old arch-enemy,

Adolf and his henchmen.

That night, GOD explained to
the Queen Mum that her work
was not finished and offered her
the chance to return to earth to
fight crime and wrongdoing.

Suddenly, the
Queen Mum
found herself
in a dark alley.

He threatened her
and pushed her to
the ground.

'Stop now!'

'You thought wrong,
young man!'

'What if everyone behaved like you?
It'd be Chaos.'

'She's got a point, I never
thought of it like that.'

'I'll go straight from now on.'
He applied for a job in a call centre . . .

'Have you ever considered
changing your gas supplier?'

And soon he was married to a grateful customer:
'I made great savings on my quarterly
bill so I married him.'

The Queen Mum celebrated with a
well-earned drink.
Before long there was a knock on the door . . .

. . . It was GOD.

'I've got another case for you.
A supermodel in trouble.
Will you take it on?'

'YOU BETCHA!'

'Just one
thing, Lord . . .'

'What are these on
my back?'

'Ah. They are the start of your angel wings. Keep going as you are and you'll have a full set by Christmas,' chuckled GOD.

'But in the meantime, don't try
to fly with them or you'll
do yourself a mischief.'

The next morning, the
Queen Mum awoke to find
herself seated in the front
row of a *fashion show*.
All the stars were there . . .

...Sid and Ethel Beckham,

Elton and David Farnsbarnes...

. . . plus the top designer **Karl Bitterbeer**.

There was a roar from the crowd as top model Shazzer Hardcastle appeared at the top of the catwalk and started to saunter towards them.

There was a glazed look in her eyes.

Suddenly, she **tottered**

and **pitched forward.**

and **wobbled**

She **fell off** the catwalk . . .

. . . and landed with her head in the **Queen Mum**'s lap.

EXIT

As quick as a knife, a
gentleman in tight trousers
ushered her backstage.
The Queen Mum
followed at a safe
distance . . .

. . . and hid behind a clothes rail.

She overheard the
man offering Shazzer
some tablets to make
her feel better.

'NO!' shouted the Queen Mum, bursting out from behind a set of designer dungarees.

'When I was your age,
I got high on life:
horse racing, dancing
the gay gordon . . .
and had no need for
artificial boosts.'

Shazzer's face changed.

'The Queen Mum
is right, I don't need this.'

She quit the catwalk and signed
up for a Highland-dancing course.
Within a week, she had landed a
lucrative sporran-modelling contract.

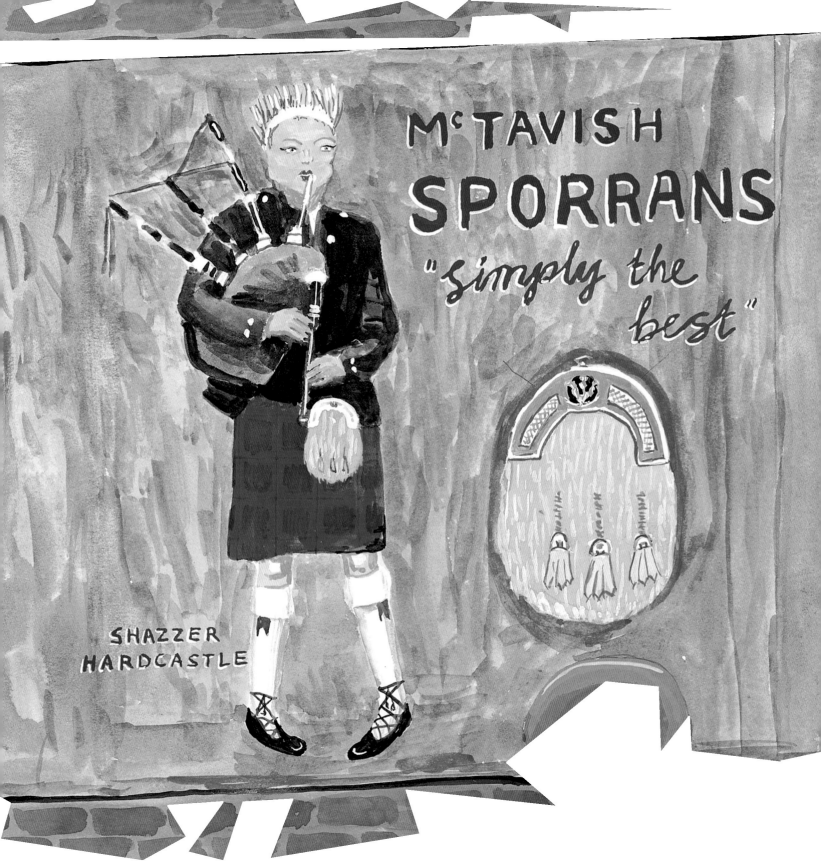

The same company approached the
Queen Mum to model argyle socks, but she
turned them down. It was a matter of *taste*.

Before she knew it, the Queen Mum was
back in her room in heaven and was about
to celebrate with her customary gin and
tonic when she thought twice . . .

. . . and settled for a game of noughts
and crosses with **Henry VIII**.

She beat him three games to nil.

The next morning, there was a knock
at the door. 'What is it this time?!!'
called the Queen Mum, knowing it
was likely to be GOD.

'Global warming!' he said.
'It's a big 'un! You'd better make your way
to reception and get the details of the case.'

The Queen Mum made her
way to reception . . .

. . . to collect the details of the case, but as
she was about to open the envelope . . .

internal mail

H.M. The Queen Mother

. . . it was snatched
from her by a tiny
lady in a nun's habit.

It was **Mother Teresa**. 'Hey, that
was my case!' said the Queen Mum.
'No, it's my case,' said Mother Teresa.

MINE!

MINE!

MINE!

'I'll arm-wrestle
you for it!' said
Mother Teresa.

They sat down at a table
and started to arm-wrestle.

First, Mother Teresa
seemed to be winning . . .

. . . then the
Queen Mum.

The Queen Mum summoned all the
strength she had and brought Mother
Teresa's arm down with a *thud*.
The case was hers.

Suddenly, the Queen Mum found herself outside the Glen Osprey Hotel, Scotland, just a stone's throw from her old stomping ground of Balmoral Castle.

The Queen Mum opened the envelope . . .

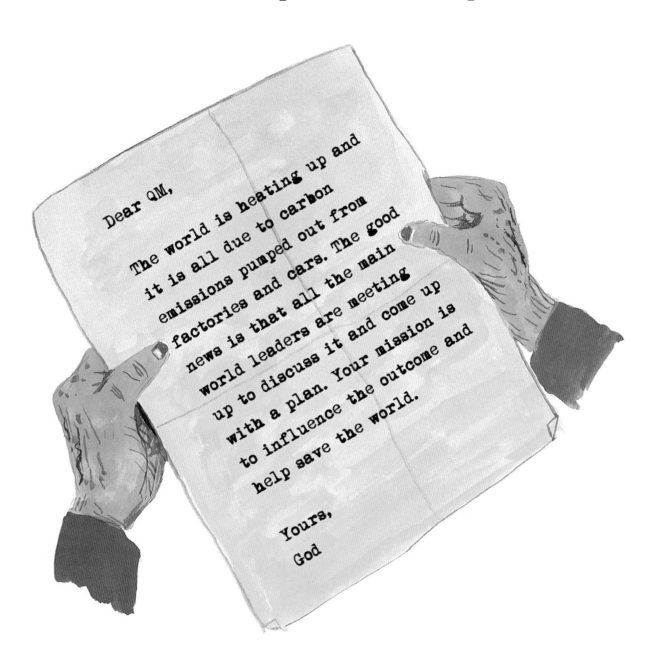

Dear QM,

The world is heating up and it is all due to carbon emissions pumped out from factories and cars. The good news is that all the main world leaders are meeting up to discuss it and come up with a plan. Your mission is to influence the outcome and help save the world.

Yours,

God

Leaders present included President
Jean Bouillabaisse of France, **Tex Oilnut**,
the President of the USA and, of course, our
own prime minister, **Nick Cheesey-Grin**. It
seemed they were all pretty much in agreement
apart from Tex, who refused to get involved.

They retired to the roof of the hotel.

The Queen Mum set about persuading
the president to sign the agreement.

As the Queen Mum was explaining the
finer details of carbon dioxide emissions
and ozone depletion, a freak gust of wind
blew the pair from the roof.

As the president hurtled towards the ground,
he had a sudden change of heart.

'Oh, if only I'd done something positive

toward saving the world, people

might remember me more kindly.'

'So you wish you'd done as I

suggested?' said the Queen Mum.

'Yes.'

Just then, from nowhere, Mother Teresa
swooped down and grabbed the pair . . .

. . . returning them safely to
the ground.
'I figured you might need
some help,' she said.

The following day, President Oilnut
signed up to help stop global warming.

He even put a wind turbine on
the roof of the White House.

Back in heaven, the Queen Mum and Mother Teresa celebrated with a ham and egg supper.

'Make friends, make friends, never ever break friends,' they said.

Then the Queen Mum discovered she
was able to flutter around the room.

THE END

Also by Harry Hill

Harry Hill

tim the
tiny
horse

He may be tiny, but he has huge ambitions